I Am Mulan

By Courtney Carbone
Illustrated by Alan Batson

 A GOLDEN BOOK • NEW YORK

ISBN 978-0-7364-4044-8 (trade) — ISBN 978-0-7364-4045-5 (ebook)
Printed in the United States of America
10 9 8 7 6 5 4 3 2 1

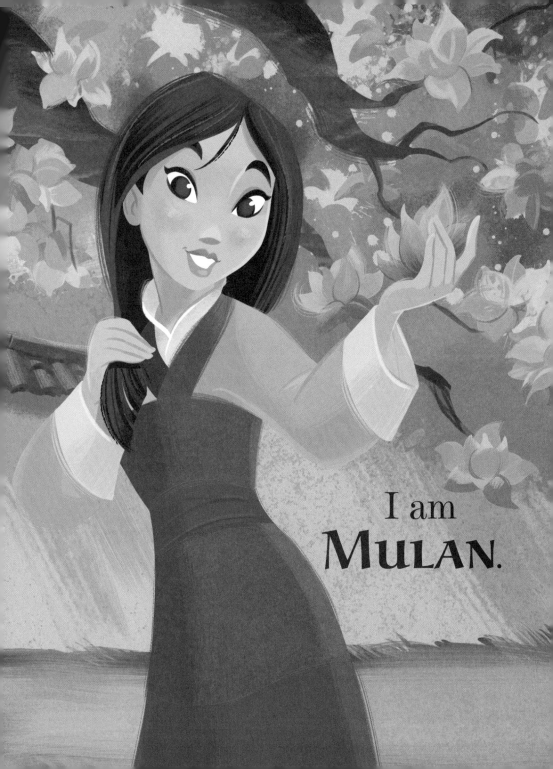

I am
MULAN.

I live in a small village in **CHINA** with my family. They are very important to me.

We have a dog named **Little Brother,**

a horse named **KHAN,**

and lots of **chickens!**

I really like **helping** others.
If someone needs a hand,
I'm always the first to run to the rescue.

Wherever I go, a **cricket** named Cri-Kee comes along with me.

He was a special **gift** from my grandmother.

Growing up, though I felt a lot of pressure to fit in, I knew in my heart that I had to follow my own path.

I wanted a life of **ACTION** and **ADVENTURE,**

and to protect the ones I love!

It was against
the law for women
to serve as soldiers.
But I came up with a
secret plan. . . .

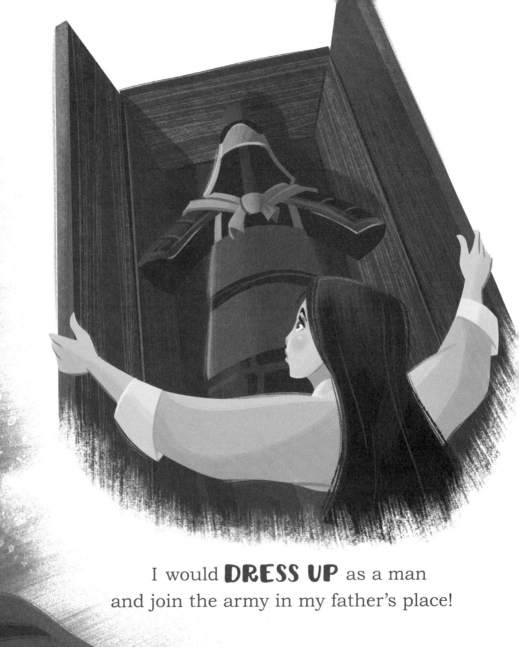

I would **DRESS UP** as a man
and join the army in my father's place!

I am very clever

and resourceful.

That helped me carry out my **plan**.

Speaking of help, I also have a

little **DRAGON** friend named **MUSHU**.

He tries to lend a hand, too, but he usually ends up causing **trouble**!

Training to become a soldier is really hard work. But I never give up!

I use my **STRENGTH** and **DISCIPLINE**
to inspire others.

I am
determined
to be the best
I can be.

I know I can do whatever I set my mind to. No one believed I could become a great **WARRIOR**.

I proved everyone wrong!

I am **BRAVE** in
the face of
danger,
just like
my father.

I jump in and take charge when
no one else will.

I also know that being a good leader means working together as a **TEAM**.

I've learned that people may
unfairly judge you because of who
or what you are. But I never let
that stop me from doing what
I know is **right**.

It feels good to earn
the **respect** of others—

especially important
people, like **THE EMPEROR.**

But what feels best is bringing **honor** to my family.

They are proud of me, and I am proud of myself.

My journey has taught me that being true to yourself is what makes you

a real **HERO!**